Radnor House

This book is due to return on or before the last date shown below

ROMANS by Ann Jungman & Mike Phillips

Bacillus and the Beastly Bath
Clottus and the Ghostly Gladiator
Tertius and the Horrible Hunt
Twitta and the Ferocious Fever

First paperback edition 2002
First published 2002 in hardback by
A & C Black (Publishers) Ltd
37 Soho Square, London W1D 3QZ

ISBN 0-7136-5959-9

A CIP catalogue record for this book is available
from the British Library.

Printed and bound by G. Z. Printek, Bilbao, Spain.

ROMANS

Bacillus
and the
Beastly Bath

ANN JUNGMAN

ILLUSTRATED BY
MIKE PHILLIPS

A & C BLACK • LONDON

CHAPTER 1

Breakages

'Now, Bacillus,' said Gorjus, 'if you are going to be young Master Clottus's personal slave, there are a few things you really need to know. He's not a bad lad, Master Clottus, there's no badness in him, but he is a very clumsy Clottus.'

At that moment they heard a crash in the kitchen and then a woman's voice scolding.

'Oh, Master Clottus, look what you've done. Another pot smashed to bits. What will the mistress say?'

'It's all right, Perpendicula. I'll tell Mother that I was the one who broke the pot. You won't get the blame.'

'That's all very fine, Master Clottus, but those Samian dishes — they have to come all the way from Gaul and they cost a lot. Now, I want you to stay out of my kitchen.'

'But Perpendicula, I like watching you cooking,' whined Clottus.

'I can't help that, young master. If I let you into my kitchen you'll burn yourself or someone else.'

'Here's a nice bit of bread and some olives — now off you go.'

Clottus sloped off feeling fed up. 'Everyone picks on me. It's not my fault that silly pot fell on the floor. It just sort of jumped. Not my fault if the pot had suicidal wishes.'

Gorjus was waiting for him. 'Master Clottus, let me introduce Bacillus. He's going to look after you now that I am a freeman,' said Gorjus.

'Hello, Bacillus,' sniffed Clottus. 'Welcome to our household, but I wish you could persuade Gorjus not to leave.'

'Come on, Master Clottus,' laughed Gorjus, 'you know that I'm not going far. I'll still be living on the estate and raising horses for your father. You can always help me break in the wild ones we bring in.'

'That's not very kind, Gorjus,' grumbled Clottus, who was terrible on a horse.

'I don't know why everyone is getting at me today. First Perpendicula and now you.'

'We're all very fond of you really, Master Clottus, particularly me, since you saved my life in the gladiators' arena. He was so brave, Bacillus! I swear, if it wasn't for this young man I'd be very dead today.'

'It was nothing, Gorjus,' said Clottus modestly.

'Why don't you show Bacillus round the villa?' suggested Gorjus. 'Then you can get to know each other at the same time.'

'Good idea,' agreed Clottus and the two of them went off together.

The first place they came to was the wine cellar. 'This is where we keep the wine,' Clottus told the slave. 'If you need to get wine you just nip up that ladder with a jug. Come to think of it, I'm a bit thirsty now. Could you get me a glass, please, and one for yourself?'

'Certainly master, it would be a pleasure,'
cried Bacillus and ran up the ladder. Clottus
leaned up against the ladder with his arm
draped round it.

'Hey, Clottus, come and look at this!' came
the voice of his twin sister, Twitta. 'We've got
a new calf.'

Forgetting all about Bacillus, Clottus ran off.

The ladder clattered to the floor, leaving the poor slave clinging to the top of the wine vat, kicking madly. Gorjus watched the whole scene from the yard and grinned to himself. 'That's my boy,' he laughed. 'That's my boy Clottus.'

CHAPTER 2

A Visit to the Baths

At supper one evening Deleria said, 'Clottus, I think it is time you started going to the baths in town with your father.'

Clottus groaned. 'Oh, Mother, do I have to? I like using the bath here.'

'That is not the point, Clottus,' said his father, Marcellus, sternly. 'You are a Roman, and going to the baths isn't just about keeping clean. It's where we meet new people, catch up with the gossip of the day, see our friends and keep fit. You are now of an age to take part and I'll expect to see you there tomorrow afternoon. Bacillus will bring you.'

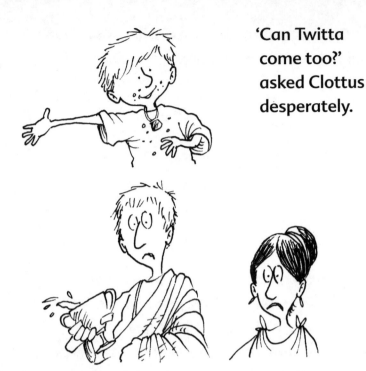

'Can Twitta come too?' asked Clottus desperately.

'Don't be so silly, Clottus!' shouted his mother and father together. 'Anyway, you know that in the afternoon the baths are only for men and boys.'

'Oh all right, then,' groaned Clottus. 'If you say so.'

So the next afternoon Bacillus and Clottus
rode into Verulamium. Bacillus tied up his
horse outside the baths and went to help
Clottus.

'Careful, Master Clottus,' he said.
'Mind the puddles.'

And he held out his arms to help Clottus down. Clottus leapt into his arms with such force that Bacillus fell over backwards into a huge puddle.

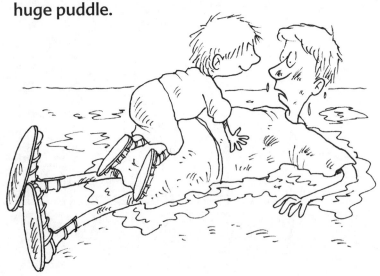

'Oh there you are,' cried Marcellus. 'I've been waiting for you. By the Gods, Bacillus! You look a terrible mess, not the way I expect my slaves to look at all! Don't let it happen again or I'll have you whipped.'

'No, master,' said Bacillus meekly. 'Sorry,' whispered Clottus.

'Let's not waste any more time, son. The first thing is to relieve yourself, so come this way and we'll go together.'

'Centurion, senator, this is my son, Clottus.'

'Pleased to meet you, Clottus. Is this your first visit to the baths?' asked the senator.

'Yes, sir.'

'You'll soon learn your way around.'

'What's the news from Rome, sir?' asked Marcellus.

'Dreadful, dreadful,' said the senator. 'Just take a look at this report, Marcellus. The whole place is going to the dogs. No discipline, that's the problem. Why, in my young days...'

Marcellus coughed and looked at Clottus.
'Are you ready to move on, son?'

'Er... yes, Father.'

'Come on, then. Good to meet you,
senator, centurion. See you in the baths.'

'I'll tell you about the situation in Rome
later, Marcellus,' said the senator.

'I shall look forward to it,' said Marcellus, as he pushed Clottus out.

'I think I may need to use the toilet again, Father,' said Clottus.

'No problem,' explained his father. 'You can use the one at the side of the baths. But when the senator starts on about how Rome is not what it used to be, well, it's time to beat a hasty retreat.'

CHAPTER 3
The Caldarium

'All right Clottus, take your clothes off and leave them here,' said Marcellus.

'Everything, Father?' asked Clottus.

'Yes, the whole lot. How else are you going to get clean? Now wrap this towel round yourself...

...and give your clothes to Bacillus. He can fold them up and leave them here in the apodyterium — the changing room.'

Bacillus took their clothes and folded them neatly.

'Right, son. The first place we go is the caldarium, the hot room.' Marcellus drew back a curtain and steam came belching out.

'I'm not going in, Father,' said Clottus nervously. 'There must be a dragon in there!'

'Well, there isn't a dragon and you are going in. Now stop making a fuss. It'll do you a power of good — you'll sweat all the dirt out of your skin. Go and lie on that slab over there and just relax.'

Clottus lay on the slab and got hotter and hotter. 'Father, how long do I have to stay here?' he panted. 'I'm getting very hot.'

'You'll just have to learn to put up with it, Clottus. You'll get to like it after a while,' Marcellus told his son.

'I won't,' grumbled Clottus. 'I jolly well won't.'

'What you need, Clottus, is a good massage,' said Marcellus. 'Xenophon, come here.'

Out of the steam emerged a huge man, with big hands. 'Marcellus Flavius, what can I do for you?' He cracked his knuckles. 'Are you ready for a good massage, sir, a really hard one, that teases out every last little tense muscle?' Xenophon rubbed his big hands together.

'No, not for me today, thank you,' replied Marcellus, 'but my son here, Clottus, he needs to be introduced to the pleasures of the baths.'

'I shall be delighted, sir.' Xenophon towered over Clottus. 'All right, young master, you just lie there and I'll do the rest.'
'I'm off into the frigidarium,' laughed Marcellus. 'I'll leave him in your capable hands, Xenophon.'

Xenophon covered Clottus in oil and then started to pummel him.

Clottus screamed. 'He's murdering me,' he cried. 'Help, help, Bacillus! Come here this minute! Bacillus, save me!'

Bacillus rushed in and looked at the huge masseur.

'Stop him, Bacillus! Hit him, go on, I command you!' yelled Clottus.

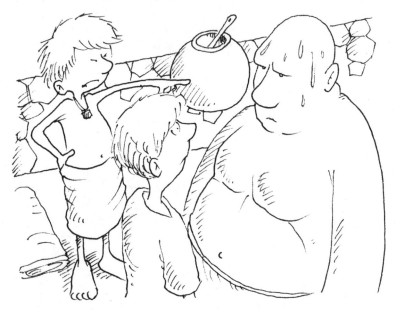

Bacillus sighed, 'Your wish is my command master,' and took a swipe at Xenophon, who punched him in the jaw and laid him out.

'Look what you did to my slave!' Clottus shouted at Xenophon. 'How dare you? I'll have you whipped!'

'I'm only obeying your father's orders, Master Clottus,' said the masseur calmly. 'Now lie still, or I'll hit you, too.'

CHAPTER 4
The Frigidarium

While Xenophon was pummelling Clottus,
who went on yelling, poor Bacillus just lay on
the floor.

Some other men came into the caldarium. 'What is that frightful noise and who is this fellow lying on the floor?' one of them asked Xenophon.

'This is young Master Clottus, sirs,' replied Xenophon, 'the son of Marcellus Flavius, and this is his first visit to the baths.'

'And the last, I hope, if he goes on making that terrible noise.'

'You stop that, Master Clottus,' warned Xenophon, 'or I'll thump you. You're disturbing the other gentlemen.'

Clottus stopped shouting. 'I hope you're going to finish soon, Xenophon,' he whispered.

'Not long now,' said the masseur.

'Could someone remove this body?' said one of the gentlemen. 'He's getting in the way. I mean, someone could fall over him and hurt themselves.'

'He's my slave,' Clottus told them indignantly, sitting up. 'He tried to save me from this torturer and got knocked out for his efforts.'

'A slave in our caldarium? It won't do! Xenophon, just drag the creature to the side, please, and make sure this kind of nonsense doesn't happen again.'

'Yes sir,' sighed Xenophon, and he dragged Bacillus out of the way before pouring a pail of cold water over him. Slowly Bacillus came round, rubbing his chin.

'Did I break anything?' asked Xenophon.
'I don't think so,' replied a dazed Bacillus.
'What made you try and thump me?' demanded Xenophon. 'I don't like hitting a fellow slave and you must have known you'd get the worst of it.'

'My new master told me to.'
'Well son, listen to an old hand. When they order you to do something daft, find a way round it. Faint, or be deaf or disappear, don't just do it.'

'Now up you get and help young Clottus into the frigidarium.'

'The what?'

'Frigidarium, the cold bath, the one they jump into after being in this hot room. You know, it's good for the skin and everything. Go on, get young Clottus out of here.'

'Come on, Master Clottus! Time to get off that slab and come into the frigidarium for a nice swim and a cooling off,' coaxed Bacillus.

'I can't, Bacillus. I'm dead. Xenophon killed me off,' moaned Clottus.

'I don't think so, Master Clottus. Now come on,' replied Bacillus patiently.

'Are you all right, Bacillus?' asked Clottus.

'Oh yes, Master Clottus! Apart from being drenched in mud, having my jaw broken and being brought round with icy water, I couldn't be better.'

'Good,' said Clottus. 'I'm glad to hear that, Bacillus, because I was a bit worried about you... now lead on to this frigidarium place.'

The two of them walked out to a large pool. 'In you jump, Master Clottus,' said his slave.

'Yes, come on in, Clottus,' called his father from the water. 'You've been hours, whatever happened to you? Come on son, just jump in! The cold feels great after all that heat.'

'You mean this pool is cold, Father? Oh no, I couldn't stand that.'

'Push him, Bacillus,' shouted Marcellus. 'I don't want a wimp for a son.'

Bacillus gave Clottus a push, Clottus grabbed hold of him and the two of them landed in the bath with a huge splash and a loud shout.

Marcellus covered his face. 'Oh no,' he groaned, 'that boy will be the death of me.'

CHAPTER 5

The Tepidarium

'Bacillus, get out of this bath! The slaves have their own washing facilities at home. You deserve to be soundly whipped.'

'No, Father,' cried Clottus, coughing and spluttering as he surfaced. 'It was all my fault, honestly.'

'Maybe you're the one who should be whipped then,' growled Marcellus. 'All right, Bacillus, go and sit in the slaves' quarters until you are called.'

'Clottus, come with me to the tepidarium.'

'Another torture chamber,' groaned Clottus.

'No, not at all,' replied his father. 'It's a warm pool and very pleasant. Look, I've brought a game of draughts for us to play in the pool for when you've scraped yourself with your strigil. Here, I'll put some oil on you, and then you scrape it off.'

'Yes, Father,' sighed Clottus.

'Don't look so miserable, son. Come on, I'll get that useless Bacillus to bring us a glass of wine each.' Marcellus bellowed after Clottus's slave. 'Bacillus!'

'Yes, master?' cried Bacillus, rushing back in.

'Wine for my son and myself, and be quick about it!' Bacillus ran off.

'Now look around, Clottus. You can see that everyone is having a wonderful time. Some are swimming, some are playing games, some are just reclining and drinking, some are discussing politics. Isn't this a great place?'

Clottus looked around him. Everyone did indeed seem to be very happy and content.

'You're right, Father. I think I could learn to enjoy all of this.'

'Of course you will,' cried Marcellus. 'And let's drink to that. Here comes Bacillus with our wine.'

'Where?' asked Clottus, jumping up and crashing straight into Bacillus, who fell and spilled the wine over all three of them.

'Bacillus!' roared Marcellus. 'You are a total incompetent idiot and you're not fit to be a personal slave! I shall have

you soundly whipped and then sent out to work in the fields.'

'Please, no, Father!' pleaded Clottus. 'It's always my fault and Bacillus gets the blame.'

'It's true, master. I know he is your son, but he is a very clumsy Clottus,' sighed Bacillus.

'Oh well, no harm done, I suppose,' said Marcellus, relenting. 'Except to my dignity and reputation. Off you go, Bacillus, and we'll manage without the wine. Come on now, Clottus, scrape off the oil and I'll pour water over you as you do it.'

When Clottus had finished, Marcellus got out the draughts. 'Come on into the pool and we'll have that game. I bet you my new knife that you can't beat me.'

'Done!' said Clottus. 'I'll just use the toilet there first.'

'Hurry up, son, I can't wait to beat you at draughts.'

'Coming, Father! I'll just call Bacillus to wash away what I've done!'

'No!' shouted his father. 'No, get one of the bath slaves to do it! Hey, slave, some water to wash away what Master Clottus has just done. Now Clottus, come down here and let's get some draughts played.'

'I'm with you, Father,' said Clottus, and he took a running leap...